For Jil – B.T.
For Leonora, Etta and Roxy – C.B.

BIG PICTURE PRESS

First published in the UK in 2025 by Big Picture Press,
an imprint of Bonnier Books UK
5th Floor, HYLO, 105 Bunhill Row,
London, EC1Y 8LZ
The authorised representative in the EEA is
Bonnier Books UK (Ireland) Limited.
Registered office address:
Floor 3, Block 3, Miesian Plaza,
Dublin 2, D02 Y754, Ireland
compliance@bonnierbooks.ie

Illustrations copyright © 2025 by Britta Teckentrup
Text copyright © 2025 by Camilla de la Bedoyere
Design copyright © 2025 by Big Picture Press

1 3 5 7 9 10 8 6 4 2

All rights reserved

ISBN 978-1-80078-712-4

This book was typeset in
Core Circus Rough and Neutraface Text
The illustrations were created digitally

Written by Camilla de la Bedoyere
Edited by Charlie Wilson and Josephine Southon
Designed by Nathalie Eyraud
Production by Giulia Caparrelli

Printed in China

THERE ARE
AMPHIBIANS
EVERYWHERE

ILLUSTRATED BY BRITTA TECKENTRUP
WRITTEN BY CAMILLA DE LA BEDOYERE

BPP

THERE ARE AMPHIBIANS EVERYWHERE

Amphibians are remarkable animals. Their name means 'double life' and many of them start their lives as small tadpoles, before going through an incredible transformation as they change into adults. While some of them are camouflaged so they can hide from predators and prey, others have brightly coloured skin.

Amphibians are water-loving creatures, so the best place to find them is around ponds and pools. All of these amphibians live on land or in freshwater. There are three types that manage to survive in salty water – which is a very special skill for an amphibian. Can you guess which ones they are?

IT'S AN AMPHIBIAN! (SO WHAT *IS* THAT?)

There are three main types of amphibians: frogs and toads, salamanders and caecilians. Amphibians are **vertebrates**, which means they are animals with a bony skeleton and a backbone. They all have moist skin, and while most amphibians have four legs, some have none!

FROGS AND TOADS

Frogs and toads belong to a group of amphibians called **Anura**. Adult frogs and toads do not have tails and their hind legs are longer than their front legs. Frogs usually have smooth skin and jump, while toads usually have warty skin and crawl.

There are more than 7,800 species of frogs and toads.

- Large eyes
- Moist skin
- Short backbone
- Large, webbed feet
- Long hind limbs

SALTWATER SURVIVORS

Did you spot the three amphibians that can be found in salty water?

Crab-eating frogs live in South East Asia. This is the only amphibian that can live in salty water all the time, even surviving in seawater for several months at a time. They eat crabs but if they live in freshwater these frogs switch to a diet of insects.

AMPHIBIANS HAVE BEEN AROUND FOR AGES

The first frogs lived on Earth around 250 million years ago, but the history of amphibians goes back even further – another 130 million years! Amphibians were amongst the first four-legged vertebrates that lived on land. Over time many species, or types, of amphibian evolved to live in water and on land. Today, there are more than 8,800 species of amphibian in the world.

Qinglongtriton

Early ancestors of modern salamanders include **Qinglongtriton**, which lived about 160 million years ago. It was about 27 centimetres long and had gills, which means it lived in water and probably resembled many modern salamanders.

380 MILLION YEARS AGO

Eusthenopteron

Eusthenopteron lived 380 million years ago. It was a large, meat-eating fish that could breathe with lungs and gills. It used its strong fins like limbs to move on the seabed. The first land-living vertebrates may have evolved from an animal like this.

The first amphibians evolved around 330 million years ago. Unlike today's soft-skinned amphibians, many of them had scales and bony plates, like a suit of armour. **Eryops** grew up to 2 metres long and looked like a stout, short-legged crocodile!

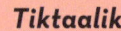
Tiktaalik

About 375 million years ago, a fish known as **Tiktaalik** used its strong fins to lift its body off the seabed and could turn its head. It may even have been able to breathe in air for a short while.

Eryops

Ichthyostega

With lungs for breathing in air and small limbs for walking, **Ichthyostega** could live in the sea and on land when it roamed the Earth around 365 million years ago.

Albanertetonids

Around 50 million years ago, many amphibians looked similar to the ones we know today. ***Prospea holoserisca*** was an early type of spadefoot toad. These modern amphibians used their big, wide feet like spades to burrow.

Albanertetonids were predators that would sit and wait for prey to pass by – using their long, sticky tongue to catch their victim. It's a handy skill that many modern amphibians still use 100 million years later.

Prospea holoserisca

Eocaecillia

Mastodonsaurus

Around 190 million years ago, early caecilians, such as ***Eocaecillia***, looked similar to modern ones, but they had little legs and did not have short tentacles below their eyes.

Over 200 million years ago, the largest amphibians to ever live were giant salamanders, such as ***Mastodonsaurus***. This mega-beast reached an incredible length of 4 metres and probably ate fish and other amphibians.

Triadobatrachus

Cyclotosaurus davidi

One of the oldest frogs yet discovered is called ***Triadobatrachus***. It could walk and swim, and probably hopped short distances. Unlike modern frogs, ***Triadobatrachus*** had a short tail. This amphibian lived about 250 million years ago.

Resembling a giant salamander with a large head, ***Cyclotosaurus davidi*** grew up to 2.5 metres long. Nearly 245 million years ago, this beast spent its life in freshwater, hunting other animals to eat.

WHERE DO AMPHIBIANS LIVE?

The place where an animal lives is called its **habitat**. Although amphibians like to stay near watery habitats, they have been able to spread all across the world, from dark caves to mountain streams and from lush tropical forests to hot, dry deserts. Some types even survive in dry habitats for most of the year but travel back to ponds to breed.

FROGS AND TOADS
Frogs and toads can be found all over the world, in both cool and warm places. Their favourite habitats are in tropical areas, where it is warm all year round and it rains most days.

POLAR PLACES
Brrr – it's too cold! There are no amphibians in the Antarctic and just five species in the Arctic. **Siberian wood frogs** have special chemicals, called antifreeze, in their blood to stop them from freezing in extreme cold.

DRY GRASSLANDS
Bushveld rain frogs live in burrows beneath the dry grasslands of southern Africa. They stay there until the rain comes, when they pop out to find food or mates before returning home.

DESERTS
It is hot and dry in the deserts of North America, where **Couch's spadefoot frogs** live. They cope with the heat by using their spade-like feet to dig a hole where they bury themselves. They wrap themselves in a cocoon made from their own dead skin to stop them from drying out, and wait there until it rains.

PONDS, POOLS AND MARSHES
Some frogs spend almost their whole lives in, or next to, water. **Northern cricket frogs** like to sunbathe on pond plants and dive into the water if they sense danger.

SALAMANDERS

Almost all salamanders live in the northern half of the world, with only about 30 species living south of the Equator. They are most common in North and Central America, especially in forest habitats.

MOUNTAINS

Giant salamanders are the biggest amphibians in the world, and they can live for up to 50 years. **Japanese giant salamanders** live in rocky, fast-flowing mountain streams.

CAVES

Olms are salamanders that live in caves, where they swim in streams and hunt small animals to eat. They have pink skin and little legs.

WOODLAND

For most of the year, **California newts** can survive away from water, living in forest habitats or grasslands. From November to December, they return to ponds to breed.

CAECILIANS

Most caecilians live in moist soil alongside streams, lakes and swamps, although a few species spend their whole lives in water. Caecilians are only found in tropical areas of the world.

RIVERS

Cayenne caecilians have lungs, but they spend their lives in water. They use a paddle-shaped tail to swim, like an eel.

HOW DO AMPHIBIANS LIVE?

It can be a challenging life for an amphibian, which might explain why there are fewer species of amphibian than any other major group of vertebrates. But amphibians are amazing animals as they have adapted incredible features to help them survive in two very different habitats: water and land.

SKIN
An amphibian's skin is smooth and covered with a slimy **mucus** to keep it moist. There are no scales, feathers or fur to protect it, but many amphibians can make a toxic skin slime, which can be poisonous to predators. Amphibians also have **colourful** skin to help them hide from predators and prey, attract a mate and control their temperature.

The skin of an **Australian green tree frog** even changes colours – it is green in the sun but it turns brown in the shade!

COLD-BLOODED
Like reptiles and fish, amphibians are cold-blooded. That means they cannot control their body temperature and will die if they get too hot or cold. That's why many adult frogs and toads hide in the shade or return to the water on a hot day.

BREATHING
While other vertebrates have lungs to breathe in air, or gills to breathe in water, amphibians need to breathe in air or water, or both. Young amphibians that live in water breathe through gills. Adult amphibians that live on land breathe using lungs and their skin, although some types keep their gills.

African hairy frogs grow special tufts of 'hair' on their legs. These tufts allow them to absorb more oxygen from water, so they can stay under the surface for longer.

Mud puppies are salamanders that can grow to 50 centimetres long. They live in ponds, rivers and streams and have feathery gills for breathing in water.

SENSES

HEARING

Frogs and toads hear using special drum-like flaps of skin. There is one behind each eye. The skin vibrates when sound hits it, and messages are sent to the frog's brain so it can hear the noise. Salamanders can hear well in water, but not in the air. Instead, they use their feet to sense vibrations in the ground.

VISION

Many frogs and toads have large, colourful eyes which can see forwards, sideways and even backwards, helping them to find food using their eyesight. Caecilians have small eyes and mostly rely on their sense of smell to find food. Frog and toad eyes come in amazing colours, and their pupils in different shapes.

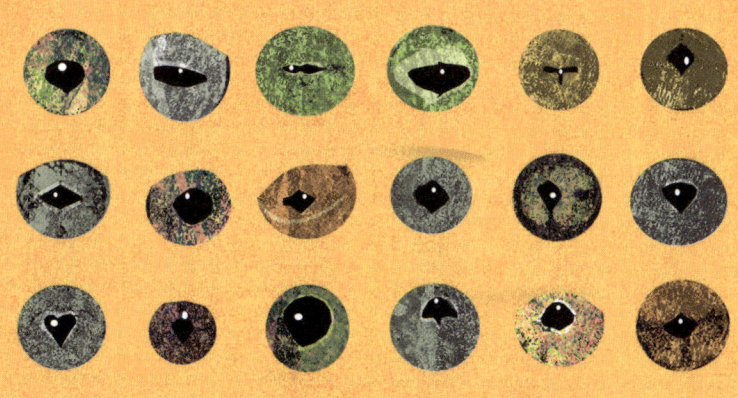

SMELL AND TASTE

Burrowing amphibians have a good sense of smell, using it to find food and mates. Some frogs and salamanders can even find the ponds where they hatched by following the scent. Caecilians use their sense of smell to find food. They have a little tentacle below each eye. This sense organ is flicked, like a snake's tongue, to detect smells and tastes.

SOUND

Male frogs and toads can be very loud! When an **American bullfrog** croaks it expands its throat like a balloon, so the noise is louder and travels further. This stretched bubble of skin is called a **vocal sac**. Males croak to call females to come to them and to tell other males to stay away.

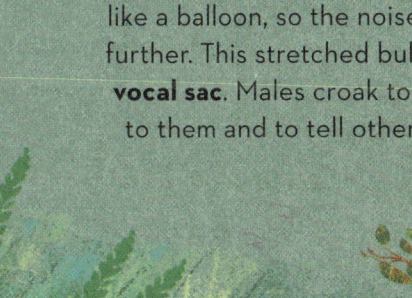

MOVING

As animals that live both on land and in water, amphibians have had to develop many ways to get around, hunt and escape danger. Young amphibians that live in water, such as tadpoles, are good swimmers, but adult amphibians have all sorts of ways to move – they can glide, crawl, climb, swim, leap and even bounce!

JUMPING
Frogs, and some toads, use their long hind legs to jump. The **sharp-nosed frog** is a champion jumper. It is tiny – about 5 centimetres long – but it can leap an astonishing 10.3 metres in just three hops!

SWIMMING
Frogs and toads use their long legs and webbed feet to swim. They draw their legs up to their body then push their legs straight out to propel themselves forward. It is the same movement that humans use when they do the breaststroke! **Webbed toes** work like flippers to make each movement more powerful.

Swimming salamanders tuck their legs against their body, and swing their body from side to side, using their tail to push forward. When they walk, they move their bodies in the same S-shape waves, swaying as they move.

Adult **northern leopard frogs** are often found hopping around on land, but when it is time to lay their eggs in water they switch to swimming instead. At this time, they can be heard making peculiar calls, which sound like chuckles, clicks and snores!

CLIMBING

Many frogs and toads can climb, where they find good places to hide and food to eat. Climbing amphibians often have small bodies but big feet with large, sticky pads on their club-like toes that grip onto the bark.

GLIDING

Amphibians can't fly, but some frogs are able to glide through the air. **Wallace's flying frogs** have flaps of skin, called **membranes**, between their toes and on the sides of their body. As they leap out of a tree the membranes stretch and spread, like a parachute, to help the frogs to soar and land gently. Gliding frogs can travel impressive distances and change direction when they are in the air. A Wallace's tree frog can leap from a height of 6 metres and travel up to 5 metres in a single glide.

CAN YOU FIND?

It's easy to see a flying frog when it is soaring through the air, but much harder to see one hiding amongst the green leaves of a tree. Can you find a Wallace's flying frog that is resting between flights?

BURROWING

Caecilians may lack legs, but they do have a strong skull, which helps them to burrow through the ground. They tense and relax their muscles in a sequence to push their bodies forward, just like an earthworm. A smooth, slimy skin makes it easier for a caecilian to slip through soil and mud.

Some species of frogs and toads are also adapted to burrow beneath the ground. These species burrow down in the soil to reach moisture, where they can remain for a long time.

FEEDING

A diet of crunchy bugs, squishy worms and other small creatures suits most amphibians. They eat a wide range of food, swallowing whole almost any creature that they can fit in their mouths – sometimes even eating their own tadpoles!

TONGUE

Frogs, toads and salamanders have long tongues that can be 'fired' out of their mouths so fast the movement is almost invisible to the human eye. The tip of the tongue sticks to the prey, and the tongue pulls it swiftly back into the mouth.

MOUTH

Amphibians have large mouths, which they can open wide to help them catch prey. **Budgett's frog** has a massive mouth for gulping down bigger prey. Like some other frogs and toads, when it is scared, it bites. This frog puffs itself up, opens its mouth and screams, while baring two little fangs on its lower jaw.

TEETH

Frogs have two different types of teeth, which are replaced throughout their lives:

- **Maxillary teeth** – little cone-shaped teeth lining the upper jaw grip and crush the prey.
- **Vomerine teeth** – located in the roof of the mouth, these teeth hold the prey still so it can be swallowed.

When the frog is ready to swallow, it shuts its eyes and rolls its eyeballs back. This pushes the prey down the frog's throat. The victim is usually swallowed whole and alive.

CAN YOU FIND?

A **Malayan leaf frog** is cleverly disguised as a dry, wrinkly leaf. It's the perfect camouflage for an amphibian that hides on the forest floor, ready to pounce on any passing bug. Can you find it?

UNUSUAL EATING HABITS

Marsh frogs usually eat bugs on the ground, but occasionally they climb up onto the backs of **water buffaloes**, where they sit and feed on the flies that land there. Up to 27 frogs have been spotted on one buffalo!

AMBUSH HUNTERS

Most frogs and toads, and many salamanders, are ambush hunters. They sit and wait for an unsuspecting bug to pass by, then gobble it up. A **Pacman frog**, which is also called an **ornate horned frog**, wiggles its yellow toes to tempt insects to come close to its mouth, before launching a surprise attack.

The **Santa Cruz climbing salamander** has a very unusual diet. Although it eats insects, it also feeds on pieces of **fungus** that it rips off the surface of a tree's bark.

CAECILIAN FEEDING

Caecilians are bigger than most other amphibians, usually reaching 30-50 centimetres long (although one giant grows to 150 centimetres). This means that while they mostly eat insects and worms, they can catch bigger prey, such as fish, lizards and even snakes.

Although a few species of frog eat plants, the **Brazilian tree frog** is the only one known to feed on **nectar** – the sugary liquid that flowers make to attract bugs. It also eats the fruits and flowers that grow on the Brazilian milk fruit tree.

LIFE STORIES

An amphibian's soft eggs are packed with goodness to help tadpoles grow, but that means they also make the perfect meal for predators, such as snakes, birds, fish and pond bugs. Some amphibians simply lay thousands of eggs, in the hope that a few of them will survive. Others have some clever ways to give their young a better chance of making it to adulthood.

DAD-DAY CARE

A male **midwife toad** gathers up the eggs his partner has laid and carries them on his back for a few weeks. If they are in danger of drying out, he returns to a nearby pond and dunks them in it! When the eggs are ready to hatch, he sits in water so the tadpoles can swim away.

PIGGYBACK RIDE

When a female **Surinam toad** lays her eggs, her partner spreads them over her back with his webbed foot as if he is icing a cake! Skin grows over the eggs, protecting them as they go through their metamorphosis from tadpole to little froglets.

WHAT A MOUTHFUL!

A male **Darwin's frog** guards his partner's eggs until they are about three weeks old, before scooping them up into his mouth. He keeps them in his **vocal sac** for about 50 days, until they have metamorphosed from tadpoles into froglets. They hop out of his mouth, ready to face the world.

HIDDEN FROM VIEW

Hiding eggs is a smart way to protect them. **Greater leaf-folding frogs** live in trees and lay their eggs on a leaf that is hanging above water. The female folds a leaf and sticks it with a glue that she makes on her body. When the eggs hatch the large tadpoles – which are up to 6.5 centimetres long – drop straight into the water.

FOAM NESTS

The jelly coats of amphibian eggs can easily dry out, so **grey foam-nest tree frogs** make a liquid, called **mucus**, which they whip up into a stretchy, sticky froth with their hind legs. It takes about six hours to make a foam nest big enough for the female to lay her eggs inside. Foam nests stop the eggs from drying out, protect them from disease and hide them from predators.

HOLLOW HIDEOUT

Eagle-eyed female **Chalazodes bubble nest frogs** search for holes in bamboo canes. They climb inside and lay their eggs, attaching them to the bamboo with strands of sticky, foamy mucus. The males then stay with the eggs, protecting them until they hatch into little froglets.

AXOLOTLS

Axolotls are salamanders that never grow up. After hatching, an axolotl spends its life as a tadpole with feathery gills. It can lay eggs without ever metamorphosing into an adult salamander. Axolotls lived in several Mexican lakes, but their habitats have been badly affected by pollution and they are now extremely rare. There may be only a few hundred of them left in the wild.

METAMORPHOSIS

A metamorphosis is a big change in body shape, and amphibians are expert shapeshifters. As they grow, they change from egg to larva to adult. While many amphibians have these three stages in their life cycle, there are some species that like to do things differently!

The **European common frog** has a life cycle that follows the typical amphibian pattern of egg, tadpole, adult.

Female frogs lay soft, round eggs in clumps called **frogspawn**. Each clump of frogspawn contains 400–4,500 eggs. A tiny tadpole, called an **embryo**, begins to develop inside each egg.

Between 12 and 16 weeks of age, the tiny tadpole has metamorphosed into a little frog, called a **froglet**. Froglets become adults when they are about three years old and can mate. They can live for up to 14 years.

BREEDING BEHAVIOUR
In spring, male frogs return to ponds, where they croak loudly to call females to join them. After mating, the females start to lay eggs. The female frog can keep laying eggs for several days. After laying, the female does not stay to take care of her eggs, or her tadpoles.

When the tadpole is about nine weeks old it looks like a little frog, with four legs and a long tail. The tail begins to shrink.

YOUNG AMPHIBIANS
Toads lay their eggs in long ribbon-like strands of jelly instead of clumps. The strands are wrapped around pond plants or rocks so they don't float away. Toad tadpoles are black in colour, while frog tadpoles are covered in gold flecks.

Some caecilian mothers lay eggs. Others keep the eggs inside their bodies until they hatch, when they give birth to their young.

STAYING ALIVE

For most animals, life is a constant battle. They must find food, shelter and mates without being eaten themselves. Amphibians are at particular risk because they are slow, small and have soft skin. They also face the danger of drying out, getting too hot or too cold. Thankfully, nature has equipped amphibians with some special skills for staying alive.

A dry, sandy desert is a strange habitat for a frog. The **desert rain frog**, however, has managed to make a home there. The short, stout amphibian digs itself a burrow in a sand dune, where it spends the day, coming out at night to feast on dung beetles. It stays moist by absorbing water from the sand, especially after a foggy morning.

If a **greater siren's** watery home dries up, it has a neat trick to stay alive. This large salamander makes itself a **cocoon** from mud and stays there – without food – for up to two years, waiting for rain to come.

In cooler parts of the world, amphibians survive winter chills by taking a long rest. They stay at the bottom of a pond or settle beneath a blanket of fallen leaves, to wait for spring.

The **ornate horned frog** copes with long, dry spells of weather by shedding layers of skin to build itself a snug sleeping bag, or cocoon, where it waits for the rain to come.

Some caecilian mothers feed their young in an extraordinary way. The **Taita caecilian** grows an extra-thick layer of skin over her body and, when the young are hungry, they bite into her skin, tearing off juicy strips to eat!

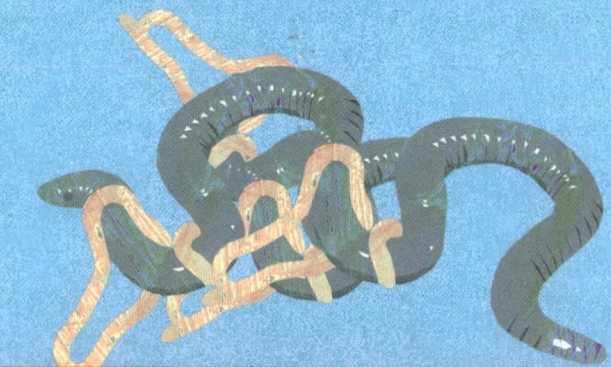

Camouflage is a great way for an amphibian to stay out of danger. The skin on this **mossy frog** perfectly blends into clumps of moss that grow on a riverbank – it is almost invisible until it hops! If that fails, it rolls into a ball and pretends to be dead.

When **hairy frogs** are scared, they break their own bones to create claws. The sharp points poke through their toes, ready to lash out and slash a predator!

The **painted salamander** defends itself from attack by spraying poison from the base of its tail. Each squirt can travel more than 2 metres and, if it hits the target, can cause terrible pain and even temporary blindness.

With its pattern of orange spots and stripes, this **crocodile newt** is warning that, like many amphibians, it tastes foul. Its warty skin is covered with a poisonous mucus that could prove fatal for any predator that tries to bite it.

Fire-bellied toads have toxic skin and flash their colourful bellies to warn predators to keep a safe distance.

TROPICAL TERRORS

Deep in the dark, damp jungles of Central and South America, there are tiny terrors lurking. **Poison dart frogs** may be small, but they pack a toxic punch with some of the deadliest poisons known to exist in the natural world. These frogs are dressed to impress, and they advertise their killer skills with bright colours and glorious patterns.

The skin of the **golden poison arrow frog** is the most poisonous of all amphibians and up to 20 times more toxic than any other poison dart frog. It is so strong that a single smear of the poison can kill large mammals in seconds.

Glass frogs defend themselves in the rainforest by using camouflage instead of poison. They create their own special invisibility cloak by being almost completely transparent. They have green bones, and their skin has a green tint, which means only the most eagle-eyed predators can spot these see-through frogs!

A **mushroom-tongued salamander** uses its sticky toes and strong, bendy tail to climb trees and hang from branches. It catches insects with its long tongue and avoids being eaten by lizards, birds and snakes by showing off its fine orange and black toxic skin.

CAN YOU SPOT?

One of the only animals to successfully hunt golden poison arrow frogs is the **frog-eating snake**, because the frogs' poison has no effect on it. Can you find a frog-eating snake as it winds through the jungle, searching for its next meal?

There are more than 100 species of poison dart frogs. They make some of the poisons in their skin, but they also use poisons that they get from eating toxic plants and bugs.

Most poison dart frogs are very small – usually just 2–4 centimetres long. They often lay their eggs in the leaf litter on the forest floor, or in water that collects inside a bromeliad plant. When the tadpoles hatch, the frogs carry them on their backs to a stream or pool.

This mighty tadpole is the larva of a **paradoxical frog**. Most tadpoles are much smaller than the adults, but in this species the tadpole reaches an extraordinary 25 centimetres long – four times bigger than the adult!

AMPHIBIANS AND PEOPLE

Most amphibians are small, shy and rarely seen. However, they have been part of human history for thousands of years, featuring in myths and legends as well as being an important source of food for many cultures. More recently, people have become fascinated by their lives, and concerned about the uncertain future that they face.

MYTHS AND LEGENDS
Amphibians have often appeared in fairy tales, myths and other stories. In Ancient Egypt, frogs were a symbol of birth and water. In Central American cultures, frogs and toads were believed to be spirits of rain. In China, frogs were thought to bring good luck. In Europe, salamanders were believed to be magical creatures that could spring to life from fire.

AMPHIBIANS ABROAD
Over the centuries, humans have travelled around the world, bringing exotic animals back with them to study and keep as pets. Unfortunately, when not controlled, these invasive species can harm their new habitat. **American cane toads** were introduced to Australia in the 1930s. Today, there are millions of these poisonous toads, damaging the natural environment.

CURIOUS CUISINE
Frogs are eaten as a source of protein due to their muscular legs, especially in Asia, the Americas and France, where frogs' legs are a considered a delicacy. One billion wild frogs are captured and eaten every year around the world. Scientists are worried that some species will be driven to extinction unless sustainable action is taken to protect frog populations.

HELPFUL AMPHIBIANS

It is important to protect amphibians because they help the world's nature to thrive.

Scientists are using amphibians to learn more about how they manage to grow new limbs or tails to replace ones they have lost (**regeneration**). The **axolotl** has been studied extensively and researchers hope they may be able to find a way to help people grow new limbs if they need them.

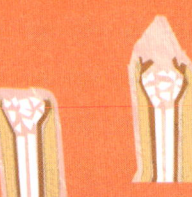
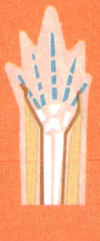

AMPHIBIANS IN PERIL

Almost half of all amphibians are struggling to survive in our changing world, with their numbers falling dramatically. Four in ten of the world's amphibians are already at risk of going extinct in the near future, and about 170 species are believed to have gone extinct in the last 30 years.

RISING TEMPERATURES

People have not been taking good care of Earth and burning fossil fuels has damaged our planet. The world is warming up, the climate is changing and the environment is damaged by pollution. With their delicate skins, amphibians are at particular risk. They struggle to cope with even small changes in temperature and moisture.

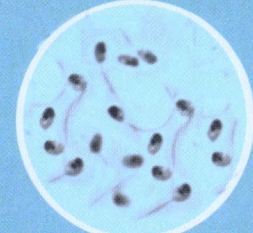

DEADLY DISEASES

In recent years, a terrible disease has been spreading amongst amphibians. Called **Chytridiomycosis** (or Chytrid for short), this disease is spread by a fungus that damages amphibians' skin. It has wiped out many populations of amphibian, and has even led to some extinctions.

HELPING HOMES

We can help amphibians by protecting their habitats. When forests and wetlands – such as swamps and marshes – are cleared to grow crops or build roads and homes, the animals that once lived there may quickly disappear.

Bug-eating amphibians are brilliant at controlling populations of flies and other insects that damage crops and spread diseases, such as **mosquitoes**.

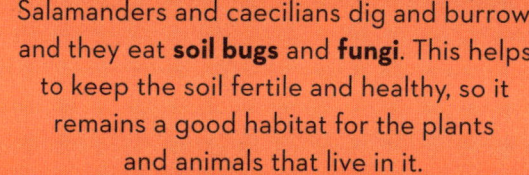

Salamanders and caecilians dig and burrow, and they eat **soil bugs** and **fungi**. This helps to keep the soil fertile and healthy, so it remains a good habitat for the plants and animals that live in it.

Tadpoles eat **pond algae** (small water plants). This keeps ponds and rivers healthy and clean, so other creatures can live there too.